This Little Tiger book belongs to:

_____

_____

_____

To Gabrielle
~ C L

For my two little mice
~ A E

LITTLE TIGER PRESS
1 The Coda Centre, 189 Munster Road, London SW6 6AW
www.littletiger.co.uk

First published in Great Britain 2004
This edition published 2014
by Little Tiger Press, London

Text copyright © Christine Leeson 2004
Illustrations copyright © Andy Ellis 2004
Christine Leeson and Andy Ellis have asserted their rights
to be identified as the author and illustrator of this work
under the Copyright, Designs and Patents Act, 1988

JUST FOR YOU!

Christine Leeson

Andy Ellis

LITTLE TIGER PRESS

Jenny opened her eyes. It was a sweet summer morning, and it was so early the sun was barely up.

"Wake up," Jenny whispered to her brothers and sister. "It's Mother's birthday today. We have to wrap her present."

All the mice jumped out of bed.

"I'll help!" cried Jenny's sister excitedly.

"We'll help, too!" squeaked her brothers.

Jenny stepped back as the mice pushed forward. "Be careful!" she cried. "You'll break...!"

SMASH!

It was too late. The present
was pulled from Jenny's paws
and shattered on the ground.

"Oh, no," said Jenny, looking at
the broken gift. "Maybe we can
find something else before Mother
wakes up. Come on, everybody!"

The mice scampered outside. Overhead, the sky
was still flushed with the pink sunrise.

"This way," called Jenny, but her older brother
had already seen something in the shadows.

"Look, look!" he shouted. "How about these?"

Next to the path there was a cluster of juicy red strawberries.

"Mm, what a treat!" Jenny said, licking her lips. "Mother will love them!"

At that moment Vole scurried out of
the dewy grass.

"Thank you," she said. "You've found
my strawberries. I was carrying some
home for my family's breakfast when I
dropped a few.

"Oh," said Jenny, feeling disappointed.
"We thought we'd found a present for
our mother."

"Maybe she'd like something else instead," said Vole. "How about those feathers?"

"Oh, yes! They'll make a nice,
soft pillow!" said Jenny, and she
scampered off to gather them.
"Mother will be so surprised. This
is going to be the best birthday
present ever!"

But just then Bluebird chirped from above,
"My feathers! Thank goodness you've found
them. I need them to line my nest and
keep my eggs warm."

"You'd better take them then," said
Jenny. "They would have made a great
present for our mother's birthday, though."

Bluebird thought for a moment. "Does your
mother like flowers?" she asked. "I can see
a pretty one in the grass just over there."
"Oh, thank you!" cried Jenny, and the
mice scurried off as fast as they could.

The grass was very tall, and the little mice
had to push and scramble through it in
search of the flower.

"I can't see it anywhere," cried Jenny.

"I see it!" shouted her little brother.

"Quick, Jenny! Over here!"

He picked up a large white
daisy and waved it over
his head. "Do you think
Mother will like it?" he
asked, stumbling under
the flower's weight.

    "She'll love it!" Jenny said.
"It will make a
beautiful present!
Let's hurry back home
before she wakes up."

Just then Rabbit hopped over. "Wait, wait!" he called. "That's my flower! My grandmother isn't feeling well, and I was going to take it home for her. I put it down for a minute, and then it was gone."

"Oh, we're sorry," said Jenny. "You should take it for her. We can find another present for our mother."

"Thank you, little mice," said Rabbit as he hopped away. "I hope you find something soon."

Jenny scratched her head. The sun was climbing over the trees into the deep blue sky. Their mother would be waking up soon and they still hadn't found a birthday present.

Suddenly something fluttered across the path. Jenny leaped up and grabbed it . . .

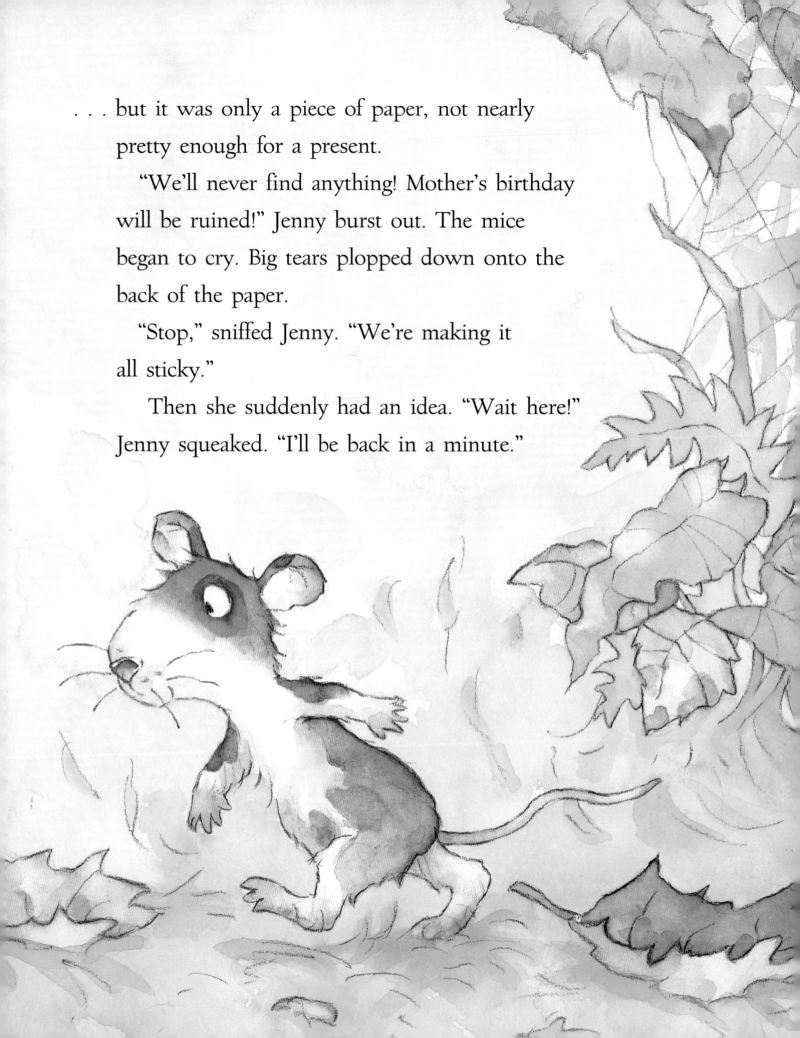

. . . but it was only a piece of paper, not nearly pretty enough for a present.

"We'll never find anything! Mother's birthday will be ruined!" Jenny burst out. The mice began to cry. Big tears plopped down onto the back of the paper.

"Stop," sniffed Jenny. "We're making it all sticky."

Then she suddenly had an idea. "Wait here!" Jenny squeaked. "I'll be back in a minute."

Jenny raced off to find Vole, Bluebird, and Rabbit. They were happy to share a little bit of the things they had found that morning, and soon Jenny's arms were full as she ran back to her brothers and sister. They squeaked with excitement as Jenny told them her plan.

Soon they were all busy, shredding and sticking, until at last the present was ready. The little mice ran home.

"Wake up, Mother! Happy birthday!" they giggled. "We've got a present just for you!"

Mother Mouse looked at the picture her children had made. It was red with strawberry, blue with feathers, and sprinkled golden with flower pollen.

"It's beautiful," she smiled, and hugged her mice close. "Thank you, everyone. It's the best birthday present ever."